Dick Hinkley

About the Author

CAMILLE NORTON's poetry and fiction have appeared in numerous small press publications, and she is the coeditor of *Resurgent: New Writing by Women* (University of Illinois, 1992). She has received fellowships from the MacDowell Colony, the Virginia Center for the Creative Arts, and the Eastern Frontier Society at Norton Island, Maine. She is an associate professor of English at the University of the Pacific in Stockton, California.

CORRUPTION

The National Poetry Series was established in 1978 to ensure the publication of five poetry books annually through participating publishers. Publication is funded by the Lannan Foundation; the late James A. Michener and Edward J. Piszek through the Copernicus Society of America; Stephen Graham; International Institute of Modern Letters; Joyce and Seward Johnson Foundation; Juliet Lea Hillman Simonds Foundation; and the Tiny Tiger Foundation. This project also is supported in part by an award from the National Endowment for the Arts, which believes that a great nation deserves great art.

2004 Open Competition Winners

David Friedman of New York, New York, *The Welcome*
Chosen by Stephen Dunn, to be published by University of Illinois Press

Tyehimba Jess of Brooklyn, New York, *Leadbelly*
Chosen by Brigit Pegeen Kelly, to be published by Verse Press

Corinne Lee of Austin, Texas, *PYX*
Chosen by Pattiann Rogers, to be published by Penguin Books

Ange Mlinko of Brooklyn, New York, *A Book Called Odile*
Chosen by Bob Holman, to be published by Coffee House Press

Camille Norton of Stockton, California, *Corruption*
Chosen by Campbell McGrath, to be published by Harper Perennial

CORRUPTION

POEMS

Camille Norton

HARPER PERENNIAL

NEW YORK • LONDON • TORONTO • SYDNEY

HARPER PERENNIAL

NATIONAL
ENDOWMENT
FOR THE ARTS

HarperCollins books may be purchased for educational, business, or sales promotional use. For information please write: Special Markets Department, HarperCollins Publishers, 10 East 53rd Street, New York, NY 10022.

FIRST EDITION

Designed by Nancy Singer Olaguera

Library of Congress Cataloging-in-Publication Data is available upon request.

ISBN-10: 0-06-079913-7
ISBN-13: 978-0-06-079913-7

06 07 08 09 ❖/RRD 10 9 8 7 6 5 4 3 2

for Maurine Stuart, Roshi (1922–1990)

and for my father (1914–1998)

In one of the first rooms I stood for a long while in front of two paintings by Shchedrin, the Sorrento harbor and another landscape of the same region; both included the indescribable silhouette of Capri, something that will always be linked in my mind to Asja. I wanted to write her a line, but I had forgotten my pencil.

—Walter Benjamin, *The Moscow Diary*

There is no evidence of salvation except a gold trace in the mind.

—Anne Carson, *Economy of the Unlost*

Contents

II *Camera Obscura*

III *Songs Against Ending*

Acknowledgments

"At the Chinese Museum, Locke, California" and "Eight Pieces for Gertrude Stein" appeared in *Field* (No. 60, Spring 1999); "Monday Music" and "Songs Against Ending" appeared in *Field* (No. 68, Spring 2003); "Savonarola's Cape" appeared in *Iris: A Journal About Women* (Fall 2003); "The Green Baize Table" appeared in *White Pelican Review* (Fall 2003) and won its Hollingsworth Prize; "The Green Baize Table" was reprinted in *Ekphrasis* (Spring 2004); "White Page of Winter" appeared in the *Berkeley Zen Center Newsletter* (Winter 2003); earlier versions of "Three Slaves by Michelangelo Buonarroti" and "The Ideal City" appeared in the online journal *She Is Still Burning* (2001); "The Ideal City" appeared in *Tiferet* (Winter 2004); and "Scattered Remnant" appeared in *Colorado Review* (New West Issue, Summer 2004). "Wild Animals I Have Known" was commissioned by Sue Johnson for her solo exhibition the Alternate Encyclopedia at the Tweed Museum of Art, University of Minnesota, Duluth, February 2004, and it is published in *Sue Johnson: The Alternate Encyclopedia*, the exhibit catalog produced by the Tweed Museum of Art, University of Minnesota, Duluth (Summer 2004). "Index of Prohibited Images," and "Paradise" appeared in *Field* (No. 72, Spring 2005).

An NEA Fellowship in poetry at the MacDowell Art Colony (2002) and two fellowships from the Virginia Center for the Creative Arts (2002 and 2003) provided space and time for the preparation of these poems.

The author thanks the University of Florence for a Visiting Lectureship in poetry in 2001.

The author also thanks the staff of the Marianne Moore Collection at the Rosenbach Museum in Philadelphia for assisting me as a Visiting Scholar in the summer of 2003.

The author gives her heartfelt thanks to Campbell McGrath for choosing the manuscript, to Stephanie Stio of the National Poetry Series, to E. J. Van Lanen, my editor at HarperCollins, and to my esteemed colleagues at the University of the Pacific for support material and spiritual.

I

Corruption

The Green Baize Table

I wanted the pear because it was green,
the same green as the baize of the banker's table
in a painting by Quintin Metsys,
The Banker and His Wife (1514)

and because it was the color of a young girl's bodice
in a portrait by Cranach,
the color of Renaissance materialism
purling over the surface of the visible.

In the painting by Metsys, the green baize table
is covered in florins, silver counterweights, and pearls
as if the table itself were the occasion for capital.

How green and planted with meaning
is the green baize table, how natural a green,
how like a pear or an apple,
a green as lush, as fertile as God's Providence
for the coming plantation of the New World.

The faces of the banker and his wife
are patient, smoothed by piety.

They are waiting for all we possess:
the traffic in things and in bodies,
the real, the virtual
heft and texture of our material.

He sits at the green baize table counting coins.
She sits beside him, turning the pages of her breviary.

But her eyes are all on him and the money

and in the Netherlandish light
one can see how much is changing,

how everything in this room is already a commodity:
the books, the pearls, the silver plate, the oval mirror
in which we can't stop looking at ourselves.

Index of Prohibited Images

AFTER CARDINAL PALEOTTI, ROME, 1597

I. John in the Wild IV, *Caravaggio, 1604*

Who wouldn't look at your lean, slouched beauty,
your shocking whiteness of body
seized inside the leafy tracing
of an obscure, dead wilderness?
You in your fur, in your red sheet,
your thighs parted and your eyes
turning away from my eyes
into your privacy, your
masculine power.

I was a boy those years I followed along the road
crying, take me, take me
into the wild, everywhere you go.
I dressed like you in suede fringed boots
and Levi jeans and muskrat fur
and a leather belt and buckle,
wanting your power, wanting to be
your Greek boy lover and you a man
wrestling me to the mat
or taking me in a field.

One night I painted you to look like a girl,
kissed you clean of the powders and shadows
by which we insinuate ourselves
into the contours of the bodies to come.
You saw through me then,

how I'd top you if I could
and tame you.

Then the other wilderness began.
I fell obscurely into my body
as all women fall when they are wild, feral.

We fought. We turned the sheets red
from the wounds. We were untamable.
We must have died then.
We didn't know how not to.

II. Judith and Holofernes, *Caravaggio, 1599*

I was nineteen when you went missing
on the road for a week with Albert's girlfriend.
I wanted to call the police, but Albert said: *Don't do that.*
The way he said it I knew you'd screwed us both and Terri too.
But we had to be cool because nobody owned nobody.

Each time you'd betray me, I'd fuck Gary, the Vietnam vet,
in revenge for your amours. I studied detachment,
read Sartre and Simone de Beauvoir in our bed.
All that wisdom and I wasn't torn yet.
I was learning to take it like a man
who parses Nietzsche between blow jobs
and lines of crystal meth.

Just when I'd begin to break down from dispossession
and the longing to possess,
I'd hear Bob Dylan singing meanly inside me:
just like a woman, just like a little girl
and I'd spring back with my girl's dagger
and cut and cut your man's mane, your blue-veined throat.

III. Medusa, *Caravaggio, 1597*

Like the boy Mario in Caravaggio's *Medusa,*
I look concave but am convex.
My face pressed against the train window
might be his face swimming behind the glass.
I'm young as he was, twenty.
The landscape streams by in tapers
of green and white and bars of black.

The moment of leaving's a gash
smeared with fixative or maybe it's memory
that rubs it flat, that leaving, those eyes
cold and glittering as a peacock's,
the hair coiled into lizards of light,
the girl's mouth crying into a declivity.

How could you fear her? She's too little.
She's only a sprite or a speck on your retina
as you stand watching from this other field
of time. The fields are lush. You
have everything she's ever wanted.
Can't you wish her well?
She's already moved past you,

and only you know where she's gone to.

Corruption

Maestro, dì, che terra è questa?

—Dante, *The Inferno*

I. The Medicis

It's late winter in Florence, nearly spring.
I'm sleeping in the shadow of the Medicis, under the eye of
  corruption.

The chapels where the princes sleep wall in my little room
as if I too were a body in the tomb of the Medicis.

At night, when the sewers run into the streets of San Lorenzo
and ripeness mixes inside the stench from the Arno,

we breathe it in, the Princes and I,

the sweet rot of the living animal,
the scent of wine and apples degrading.

Lorenzo the Magnificent. Cosimo the Elder. Piero the Gouty.
How they loved the rankness of the human body.

Don't be fooled by the figures on their tombs:

Dawn and *Dusk, Night* and *Day* by Michelangelo,
giants marbled in tomb light, resembling

us, dissembling us.

Michelangelo's bodies are incorruptible.
Bigger than life, more beautiful than we are

but not more real.

The Medicis were real. The Medicis had ambition.
They overreached and died young.

Don't you hear them sighing in the darkness?
It's as if you're listening to your own mind

breaking down, breaking down
into a human echo.

II. The Monsters

Pity the monsters! Pity the monsters!

—Robert Lowell

Ten years ago I would have hated you.
Now I find you funny and kind.

I forgive you your cigars.
You think you can read me and you're wrong.

I like that you're wrong about women.
It makes me feel smarter and more erotic than you are.

And I like the way you take my arm
when we walk after dinner, late, in the old city,

the Quattrocento unfolding on either side
of the Piazza Signoria and not a soul but us

to mark the spot where they burned Savonarola.
The light's smoky this time of year, almost witchy,

a kind of light that flatters and conceals
the edges we don't like about ourselves.

We talk about the dead we have in common,
famous poets in the hills, men who pitied monsters

and themselves, never their children or their wives.
We loved them anyway, but why

unless we're monsters too.
Never mind. It's late. Console me.

Show me Perseus and the head of his Gorgon.
Judith and the head of Holofernes.

It's a dead heat in the gender wars and nobody's winning.

You tell me about a girl you like, the one you're courting
in your hotel, a chambermaid of incomparable

ripeness. She's twenty-five, you're sixty.
You say that when you gaze into her eyes

you can see *she's already been corrupted.*
You relish the word the way you relish the female body.

Corruption. There is no pleasure without sin.
The idea, like you, has a kind of charm.

Old seducer, you're neither my father nor my lover.
Neither of us is as corrupt as we pretend to be.

What are we doing walking together in the dark?

III. The Saints

for Elisabetta Borghi

He must have died in the cloister, in a cell with a barred window
and a new fresco by Fra Angelico painted on the wall.

When he died, his mouth fell open into an O and a little bird
  flew out
soundlessly. His soul, they say, flying through the bars.

The year was 1459. The dead man was Fra Antonino Pierozzi,
a Dominican, the founder of San Marco.

He's still here, in a glass case near the sanctuary,
a permanent installation in the left aisle.

How tiny he is, Fra Antonino.
He's brown as a nut and shiny and leathery.

His skin's so tight you can count the bones of his face.
He has what they call *an uncorrupted body.*

Some women have uncorrupted bodies but not many.
Catherine of Siena. Saint Lucy maybe.

Most women prefer to disappear when they die,
out of compassion for children and an instinct for beauty.

Not Fra Antonino.
His feet poke out through his golden booties,

his mouth's agape in its terrible O.
He's breathless and he can't let go.

Imagine growing up looking at men like him,
the undead dead in every village church in Italy

and you are young and beautiful and on the threshold
of all you cannot keep, a hundred pleasures.

Savonarola's Cape

EXECUTED IN FLORENCE IN MAY 1498

How to explain my fear of Savonarola's cape,
spread flat as bat wings on the cloister wall

above his pitiful rope bed and pitted breviary?

My fear of his great hooked nose, his black eye
trained like an eagle's on the female body's

lushness, on Neoplatonism's
lust for boys, on the obscene Pope's

hunger for things, things.

He died by rope, he died by fire.
The river's deconstructed his voice

and all that remains of Savonarola
remains in these two cells

at the end of the cloister of San Marco,
a cloister pure as honeycomb

in the way it divides silence
among the whitewashed rooms.

Here one could contemplate for thirty years
a single fresco by Fra Angelico

and still not have penetrated the mystery
of all that suffers like you,

of all that redeems through the body.

And in that silence, what grace.
Even now you can feel it

as you move through corridors
rubbed soft with beeswax,

listening to the sound your body makes
traveling in and out of emptiness.

What could prepare you for the body in pain,
the screw holes of self-flagellation,

the worm-riddled shroud of his terrible cape
tacked in the air, the narrowness of his bed,

the littleness of his chair.

And what a world to fall into.
A world like a text spilling across the mind,

or like a voice, dispossessed, half-articulate,
no telling now who it belongs to

as you hear it, as you choose how not to hear it,
and you will always have to choose

as you move back through cloisters
of honeyed cells

into the wash of light,
all the sweetness.

Three Slaves by Michelangelo Buonarroti

C. 1530, AFTER THE GALLERY OF SLAVES,
GALLERIA DELL'ACCADEMIA, FLORENCE

I. The Young Slave

A slave is not born but made, as women are made
in those fabulous narratives of Ovid.
You know the stories: the metamorphosis
of girl into fish, girl into fowl.
Mermaids in the sea, nightingales
in the trees, circling, circling
with menace and sorrow
the loss and the lack,
the improbable riddle
of what women want.

This slave could be a woman,
but he's a rent boy on his knees.
The master's chisel marks the place
of sufferance, and now, running your hands
along the cuts, surreptitiously, in the gallery,
you can feel the master's intention
to make stone speak as if it were a body.
His body or the boy's
caught in what net of desire,
in what transaction?

The boy's unfinished.
His genitals rise, his tipped nipples
lift away from the master's hand.
You're there to look at him and so you look

at the prison of his beauty,
at the way he is neither subject nor object
but both incompletely,
as if he were practicing in front of a mirror,
imitating that look
we call femininity.

Master. Slave. Slave. Master.
All along the traces of his young body.
All along the traces of her young body.

O take me.

II. The Awakening Slave

It's not easy to wake when sleep is sweeter than reason.

Consider the light surrounding Giorgione's reclining Venus,
its muted russets and tempered golds, its soft green

mosses, its umber road
unfolding sensuously inside a world of shadow.

As Venus sleeps, her hand caresses
the cleft beneath her pubic bone.

Who could wake her?

In *The Awakening,* by Kate Chopin,
Edna Pontellier startles awake from a life of pleasure

and drowns herself within the year.
A kind of erasure it seems to me, though my students say, no

she is free and besides, we're all slaves, Professor.

But wisdom lies in the awakening of the entire soul
from the slumber of its private wants and opinions.

To see the world whole, apart from oneself.
To love the world anyway, for its own sake.

But how many ever do?
And what about the danger

of awakening partially or halfway
like Michelangelo's half-hewn man

hurtling inside his marble trace
half in, half out like a moth trapped in a chrysalis.

He's running in place.
What's worse, he's running in place for all eternity

and he knows it because he's awake
after the long dream of passage

in which he's always racing forward into shadow
or back into the sweetness

of night falling in a dark blue meridian
that is elsewhere and in between

the waking body
and the dream.

III. Atlas

The slave we call Atlas is attached to an unshaped immensity.

Atlas lived in Atlantis once.
Now he lives in the Gallery of Slaves at the Academy in Florence.

There's a block of stone where his head should be.

Unlike David, who has a head wrapped in acanthine curls,
a slingshot, buttocks, and inescapable genitals,

Atlas has only the burden of the material against which he
    struggles—
raw marble, a torso, one shoulder, one heroic arm.

His arm pushes mightily against a dead weight
and disappears inside it, as if weight itself had a secret chamber

where one could think things through, away from the crowd.
His head's in there too, thinking

of mind over matter or matter inside mind or the other way round.
Big Mind is like a sky vault or like a mountain,

hard to support with the head alone.
And yet one needs a head to figure out

how mind attaches to the stuff we're made of.

Atlas attaches through tendon and nerve.
Atlas has a spinous process.

Atlas is the first vertebra of the cervical spine.
Atlas is a winged bone with a hole in it.

Atlas is delicate.
Atlas curves and breathes

up through the hole to the great sky dome
where the Pleiades light up the dark and private life

of the mind, where we are all of us alone.

The Ideal City

ANONYMOUS, C. 1475, TEMPERA ON PANEL,
GALLERIA NAZIONALE DELLE MARCHE, URBINO

for Maurine Stuart, Roshi (1922–1990)

After a long exile, the city of the mind must look like this—
placid because uninterrupted by what happens next

and therefore pleasing, pleasing and empty.

Here the light clicks across the white and gray
Carrara marble and pietra serena

going nowhere, intending nothing.
It is beautiful. It is itself.

Light then, light as it breezes through
vacant piazzas and quiet loggias,

light as it unravels,
illuminating interiors where no one lives or dies or loses ground.

Light as *a systematic display of single point perspective*
hastening now around the columns of a rotunda

then slipping through a small red door
into the refuge of a stanza.

All your life you thought of such a room and then you found it.

When a woman starting up from the sensible world
catches sight of beauty, she should not look back

at all she used to love. Her body moves
into a light so absolute it casts no shadow.

Nobody here, nothing to do, you said in your hospital bed.

Then you disappeared.

In the Small Refectory

AFTER DOMENICO GHIRLANDAIO'S *LAST SUPPER* (1480),
MUSEUM OF SAN MARCO, FLORENCE

The season of last things.
Florence that summer the Master loved you.

The long table in the breezeway,
a scattering of hazelnuts and round panini,
some flasks of wine and water

and you, John, asleep by a soft green
alabaster bowl the color of moss,
your golden head at rest in your arms,
the breath of the god upon you.

Outside the window, a whir of pheasants' wings
seems to mix into the inside sound
of the room, voices breaking like waves
against the dream in which you are
always a boy, always at the threshold.

But what does it matter now?

You sleep inside a world of signs
too finely etched to alter.
The line of cypresses: *death of the man you love.*
The peacock at the window: *promise of resurrection.*
The lustrous eyes of the little cat: *enemy of the Lord.*

The Judas look crosses the room.
Your hand curls inside the folds of your blue sleeve.
Light falls against your skin as if it loves you.

Later, when you no longer remember
the last afternoon you slept between his knees,
when you've forgotten how he looked
and how he touched you
and why it was that you followed him everywhere,

they'll say about you:
He was always the last to see.

What did he ever have besides youth?
What did he ever have besides beauty?

Napoleon's Boots and Dante's Body

Dante slept for a long time in the nineteenth century, thanks to
  Napoleon,
a little man in tall boots with a genius like a corporation's

genius for acquiring other corporations.
Little Napoleon marched into Italy, tiny Napoleon consumed
  the Church

as if it were the antipasti. And there's nothing like antiquity
to make you hungry for the treasures of a tomb.

Ah, what a tomb was Italy: Etruscan, Roman, Arian, Byzantine,
medieval, Quattrocento, neoclassical, rococo—

all beautifully elided like layers of pastry in a papal cannoli.
This is so good I must eat the whole thing, said Napoleon.

That is how law works to bring appetite and things together.
Napoleonic Law or Natural Law or the Law of the Father
  depending

on the body of law you study in school. But back to Dante,
dying in exile, in Ravenna in 1321, buried

at the Chiesa di San Francesco, dug up in 1519, smuggled out
through a hole in the wall by faithful Franciscans

in the struggle with Florence, *that faithless mother,*
hidden awhile in the windy plains near Ferrara,

then shut up at last in a wooden box
in 1677 by Padre Antonio Santi.

So many hells of sanctuary had Dante.
He was as hunted as a saint.

Would they never stop?
It was quiet again all through the eighteenth century,

but then, Napoleon, a little man in tall boots,
an arriviste of the worst kind, the kind that wants it all—

your dead, your living, your perversions, your convictions,
your painting, your poets, your prelates and pretty girls—

wanted Dante's body too
and would have had it, if not for the faithful Franciscans

scuffling in the night, digging, digging
a pit in the soil of Braccioforte,

a pit of such excellent, hermetic silence
that even they forgot where they had put it.

So it was that they lost his body.
And so it was that Dante got free.

And Dante slept for half a century,
his lost body traversing the underground source of the lyric

phrase of the wind as it traveled across him
in the tall grasses

in the tall grasses of Braccioforte.

Paradise

I. Itzá Historian, Tayasal, Guatemala, 1525

Cortés rode a wounded horse, Cortés the god.
We have not come to kill you, he said.
Let us rest with you awhile in this green shade.

Our brothers had run away, fearing the plague
of whiteness, the hairy faces and flaming crosses
of the cavaliers, but Cortés, Cortés

played for us on trumpets of gold and bone
like thunder before rain, like our god Chac
who makes the storms, and Cortés's little tapir

of a horse sat on the ground like a woman
bleeding from her womb. When he left her behind,
we fed her flowers, iguanas, and cooked turtles,

but she could not live without him.
And so we built him a new horse we called
Tzimín Chac, little horse and god of thunder,

and we put her in our temple and worshiped her.

II. Father Urbita, Tayasal, Guatemala, 1618

I entered this green hell rife with idols,
stone faces at the top of stone stairs
and a statue of a horse sitting like a devil

on the ground, in *no known equine posture,*
shaped like a human or like a woman
unnaturally hung with teats, covered in flowers.

How not to be filled with *a holy rage*
how not to seize a stone tablet in my hands
and smash to pieces the animal they adore?

The Indians swarmed over us with terrible faces
of cut stone, crying unintelligibly in the fiery tongue
they use among themselves, but Father Fuensalida

preached at the top of his voice and they let us go.

III. Itzá Historian: Arrival of Father Delgado, Tayasal, Guatemala, 1622

This Delgado had a fur face like the two who killed our god.
He wore the hair skirt and the beads, like them,
and carried the cross and came singing out of the forest

with eighty of our kind whom he had bewitched.
We greeted them joyfully with blind smiles
and waited for them to make music for their god

in the gathering place where they plant the cross.
We came on them then and tore out their hearts
but we did not eat them for fear of the poison.

We burned their hearts and buried them, we fled
far into the heart of the world where the tapir feed,
where the thunder gathers to make the rain

and where no white men ever come.

The Africans of Ravenna

In Ravenna, they sleep in the Cistercian cloisters
inside double porticos of fifteenth-century stone
and in coffins of cheap cloth,
their mummy bags lined up in rows,
their things in piles:

boom boxes, blue packages of Gitanes,
pairs of Nike knockoffs laced together
in a corral of dream.

A little winter light drizzles down
all morning as the tourists walk around them
to peer disconsolately at the Tomb of Dante.

At night, in the vaults below an ancient oratory
where a prophet lies buried,
their voices sing along the old sarcophagi,
calling out, *Venez ici, mes frères.*
Nous avons du potage, un peu de vin pour vous.

Strangers. What port out of Kinshasa brought you here
by way of Genoa and the train from Milan?

You are miles inland from the gray Adriatic's
floating tankers and stowaway freighters.

How will you ever find your way
back into the epidemic of time?

At the Chinese Museum, Locke, California

> *Of all the changes of language a traveler in distant lands must face,*
> *none equals that which awaits him in Hypatia, because the change*
> *regards not words but things.*
>
> —Italo Calvino, *Invisible Cities*

A dead woman's trousseau. A baby's linen shoe.
Racks of rice bowls and ladles, tin pots, brass bells.
A bachelor's opium pipe, a gambler's nicked tiles.
Nobody's things, belonging to nobody now.
A girl's red quilted jacket, item 39,
mildewing on the aluminum hanger. Her letters home.
Sheet music from Canton, songs about snow.
The news from Sacramento, 1902, photographs
of field laborers and drowned brides.
Cook and Auntie in starched white jackets
counting baskets of strawberries and asparagus.
Riverboats unloading cornmeal, cotton, the bright clot
of blood in the water. The stench of cattle
and bodies from the lower deck.
The smell of sick in the canal.

Slow inland river, sweet rot
of oranges, camellias, soil, shit
and Al the Wop's Special,
your river gods go for eighty bucks a pop,
a pair of faux coolie pajamas, permanent press,
with I-Ching coin buttons and snap fly—for somewhat less.

At the Chinese school, in the bad light,
two pages of a primer, creased as goatskin

and blue with mold, translate signs into cursive.
The change regards not words but things,
and not proper names but nouns
that neither wound nor shame you:
money, waiter, fork, spoon.
Diction of the restaurant.
The children have disappeared.
The invisible uncles keep still.
They'll have nothing to do with you.

Still Life with Oranges and Walnuts, 1772

AFTER LUIS MELÉNDEZ, NATIONAL GALLERY, LONDON

A relief to turn away from the world,
to sit at a table weighted with the spoil of winter's
blood oranges and black walnuts, amid great round wheels
of cheeses, the terra-cotta jars of olives
that are dark and oily, a little smoky
on the tongue, for you have tasted them
on the sly, haven't you
unsealed the mouth
of the jar, slipped your fingers into the alluvial
secret place in the crescent of its body?

It's what you've done all these years without sex,
tasting one thing and then the other,
the split melon, the unwrapped
sweetmeats, wine, and bread,
a little fizzy water,

returning to your senses in a private room
outside of history, so it seems,
at this table, with this larder's
darker pleasure,

recompense for all the losses of age
and ordinariness, for being merely human
like all the others

like yourself

in a life that is fertile, still.

II

Camera Obscura

Incomprehensible Triangles

for Jo Smail

Will I stay lost amid the silence of the signals?
I will for I know what I'm like: I never learned to look
without needing more than just to see.

—Clarice Lispector

They unfolded all around me but I could not read the pattern,
the way love opened to include the third term,
the way love swallowed a boundary,
the edge of her body or his,
how one was never alone with another person,
but always in concert with the one who came before,
sometimes a mother or a father,
or the dead self, the younger body
that is never dead at all, only mute.

Sometimes there is around a scene a kind of halo,
and one sees for a moment all that is never said.
Inside the silence of the signals there is a field of light.
It takes years to stand inside that clarity
without reaching for another language.

Standing quietly I know I've failed to speak directly about love.
I could never hold it long without fleeing its implication.
To love a person, you must take her entirely:
the darkness of a girl, her hinged history,
the third term of the wound or the dream,
which is the halo and the silence of the signal.

Oh, incomprehensible,
can I bear you one more time, this love
at the perimeter of all I know and all I fail to know?

Camera Obscura

*the origin of errors in vision must be sought
in the conformation and functions of the eye . . .*
— Johannes Kepler, 1604

The feeling mind was like a mirror,
the origin of errors, this crooked mind
getting everything backward:
the sign and the signified, the alphabet,
the left shoe and the right shoe.
My cotton shoelaces would not pull tight.
The knots were bad. They came undone.
The leather tongues flapped
in the mouths of my red oxford shoes
that were the color of cow's blood.

My eyes were pinholes. I was too shy to see
with a wide lens and so I looked covertly
at the trees growing out of the sky's blue pool,
their massy green roots quivering in sunlight
as they grew backward into the earth,
piercing the crust of the world with their trunks,
disappearing into an underground of cold springs
and granite cracks that I could see obscurely
as if in a mirror slightly bent backward.

When I looked down I could see
straight into the heart of a scene, only in reverse,
so that I saw history first, then the transfer
of the present bleeding through the pinholes
like light on the screen of my mother's face,
the way it settled unhappily there,

pushed forward by the years she had lost
to my errant father, who was always sleeping it off
or otherwise was absent from the scene,
though I could see him too, in the mirror,
the way his body had worn out the young man
and covered his beauty with fatigue.

I saw them and I saw them indirectly
the way I saw a world of truth and error
in a mirror shield, in my curved and beveled mirror
that was as inexact as any eye,
as inexact as any picture.

Aperture

The night my father died the salt and the rain went out of him

leaving behind a reverberation
like sunlight skimming through glass

It was like that just after
and for some time
it was like that

like light behind film strip, a ticking mutability in everything
left behind on the nightstand, it was so little, it was nothing
in the way of effects
                      He had nothing to leave us—

his poor man's watch winding down imperceptibly in its steel case,
the narcotic trace in empty pill cups, nine copies of his brother's
face on nine 1987 Mass cards, his radios, his radio batteries,
his hearing aid (despised, cast off, it never fit),
The Philadelphia Inquirer folded at the spine as he would have
  folded it,
his white cotton handkerchiefs, clean and triple-creased—
he did not die penniless, exactly—

the object world had survived him
                        And it was animate

Animate with its own disappearance
as if it had bubbles in it, tiny apertures
and pinpricks of negative space
through which we would all disappear sooner or later

Why this should console me I cannot say but it did
and I knew, even as I stood in the door of his closet,
that when the scent of his shirts began to degrade
I could do nothing to stop it
though I must have thought I could follow it as if it were

a thread
leading to the other side of matter
where the problem of matter is repaired

They say that you should not importune the dead
too soon in their dying

because they go on dying awhile elsewhere

But one night soon after we buried him,
while I lay sleeping in my father's bed,
I knocked at his dream and entered it

He seemed surprised, as if I were an acquaintance
who had climbed the stairs on a whim, without invitation
He was sitting mildly on a small chair in a clean blue shirt
He was young and slim, my bachelor father, he was unaware
that he was young and slim, that his hair was black
as a pirate's, that he would ever grow old or that I
would ever be born
Until he said: *I'm dead, can't you see that?*
Get away from here And I was out, out with a force

I trespassed and survived it

Then my sister's hands were on me.
She was warm, she smelled of chocolate
She brought me water in a bathroom cup
that had ridges in it from where it had melted
in the dishwasher a long time ago
We talked ourselves to sleep, we slept
past the broad stripes of July sun
ticking across the pavement
We slept all afternoon
                              and when we woke
the surface of the world had slipped
and locked into place
between our bodies and the myriad portals
through which *the branching streams
flow in the darkness.*

Gorgias

Gorgias wrote that when we think about nothingness
we cause it to exist as a quantum in the mind.
Or maybe Gorgias wrote that the world does not exist
apart from the mind.

But what is nothingness if it exists?
And what is the world if it does not?
Is *what is not* something that never was
or is it something that has ceased to be?

My father has ceased to be and so have my red shoes.
My cat of nineteen years, skulls and spines
I found in fields, a cow's head once, bony things
that fell apart and seemed to disappear but only seemed.

Even they had too much return in them and too much time.
If it's nothingness you want you have to let go of resurrection.
Ah, Gorgias, *what is not* is an oblivion in which the verb *to be*
  unravels.
It's the milky cloud whirling inside my mother's mind
or a vortex with the north wind in it carrying her away.
It's my mother growing unrecognizable.
It is what I cease to see when I see her,
body without mind or anyway mind without a place for me in it.

Mind without world, without self, without the dreams of the self
she must have dreamed all those years before I came to be
someone she named after a film. Or was it a novel?
Now my mother cannot say *mine, mine*

and that is something and that is nothing at the same time.

In the Bardo

for Jane Picard

I. The Bardo of First Things

I'm thinking about the hummingbirds in the tree behind you.

What do you think about when you see hummingbirds?

I think about their shadows whirring against the acacias.
And I think about the first hummingbird.

Where is the first hummingbird?

In Maine, on a logging road near Mount Katahdin.

It has a ruby throat.
It startles me now like the shape of bliss.

Like something unimagined that is suddenly there?

Like something unimagined.

I'm six. I am wearing a red coat.
My mother walks ahead of me on the road and she is sad.

And for a moment I look away from my mother
and see the hummingbird,

a slashing green jewel of a bird cutting between
my body and my mother's body

like an arrow from the bow
like the knife of happiness.

II. The Bardo of the Dream

You're in the still point where breath moves through the body.

It's the middle of the night
and you're forty or maybe fifty

and you have no idea where you are.
You feel like you're falling far.

You feel like you have no story

apart from light crossing a room
apart from breath crossing a body

lengthwise like the ingress of an estuary
pouring in and out of the sea.

The sea pours in and out of an estuary.
Is it marshlight or starlight now?

What part of it do you belong to?
What part of you belongs to me,

bitter, beautiful woman?
Spit on the ground.

Come back to your body.
Your own mind's shining before you,

all that willfulness, bad temper,
all that toughness carried lightly.

III. The Bardo of the Mind in Contemplation

Why did you go this way and not another?

There wasn't enough silence, not enough rain.
Not enough balm. Not enough gratitude.

Not enough forgiveness?

I wanted to be taken in as I was.
I wanted to be a child a little longer.

Not enough sweetness?

Where I lived you're all grown up at twelve.
After that they say you deserve what you get.

Nothing tender?

I walked into the woods and some boys got me.
Then I started slipping out of the world

and I kept on slipping.

Where are you going now?

I don't know.

What do you have to show for yourself?

Only this.

Is it enough?

It's never enough.

Do you want to come in?

I want to come in.

IV. The Bardo of the Dead

World is a leaf and a little wind
World is a feather

World is the mind crying out

And so I listened
World is a leaf and a little wind

World is a feather
World is a wishbone and a little skin

I had a mother I had a father
I had a mind crying out

And so I listened

Someone was climbing
and then someone was falling

I had a leaf and I had a father
I had a father who kept falling down the stairs

I had a mother I had a mind crying out
I had a father and I had a feather

I had a wishbone and a little skin
I had a reason I had a world

And so I listened

I had a leaf and a little wind

Thirst

. . . *the drunkard is not aware of where he is going*
because his soul is wet.
—after Heraclitus

Little amber bottles, then empty fifths—
the drowned state of one who has lost her senses.

Her soul is wet. And so she drinks.
We step and do not step into the same river.

Is there a universe in which we choose such things?
To drown or drift? To burn in a ring of fire?

At night I listen to the minute chinks
of ice against her glass as I drift to sleep.

The drunkard has lost her way. The temperate
can never say how or why the drunkard got that way.

Heraclitus says that the souls of the good
are composed of warm, dry air, a kind of summer.

The olive trees ripen. The sea is there.
And she is our mother.

But what of the others whose souls are wet?
Thirsty ghosts in search of something strong and bitter.

Are they bad? Are they wrong?
Are they sick? Will they get sicker?

We're born in moisture, enclosed in thorny barks,
writes Anaximander. *Then we come forth into the drier part.*

But sometimes we arrive in a fever, eager to slake
heat with brine, thirst with dirty water

and if we choose, what do we choose—
the manner of our arrival or of our departure?

The Mirror Stage

I. Foolish Girl, Counting the Days

Foolish girl, scaring yourself in the mirror.
How you have aged.
Almost fifty and fat as your mother
before Prempro and the gym saved her
for a svelte old age of international travel.
You're haggish with worry now, you wonder
when you began to unravel
sex from the bed you made
when you were young enough to be Byronic
and bisexual and still get laid
by dark angels and ironic
strangers with advanced degrees.
There must have been a moment.
Can you locate it? A dark swerve through trees,
a kind of fall or dull plummet

down into the body you became.
Oh, suddenly this body and only yourself to blame.

II. I Dreamed Last Night I Had a Date with John F. Kennedy

The father of course, always the father, never the son.
I wore the dress I always wore to the symphony
when I was twenty in Philadelphia, or twenty-one.
In the dream, I stood idly in my best black crepe,
waiting, like Marilyn, for the call that never came.
Oh, dreamland, dreamland, the drift and shape
of my desire to screw the president and stake my claim
on the father, all of this dates me horribly,
the contradictions and conflicts of the imaginary,
the gaps and rents in my feminist ideology,
and the pathos of the body tucked into history's
cartoonish abyss. Shall I tell you what happened next?
I stripped off the dress and went swimming with the son,
not the dead son of the dead president, but a high-sexed
nautical boy who swam alongside me like a dolphin.

We made a sorrowful pair as we scissor-cut the water,
for he was the father's son and I was my father's daughter.

III. I Suppose They Call This Menopause, the Way I'm Flashing Off and On

with utterance. I have these several voices
I can't repress, haggish voices without melody, long-
winded voices that carry on about choices
I've made about love, how I could never decide
between men and women, chose sad marriages, failed to
   commit
to matrimony, pursued the mind and found a place outside
the body, inside the mind-body split.
Oh yes, this is the age of regret
and I musn't mind my svelte mother's telltale rejoinder
that I have made this bed and that I will not get
another. Oh, my mother, you can't say she didn't warn her,
that girl I was, bookish and obtuse about the mirror,
which so lately scares me like a fate.
I'm forty-eight and I hear my mother
in the well of my bed, like a bellwether rising late

from the dream of loneliness:
You chose this, you chose this.

Subterranean

I. Joseph Le Conte at Soda Springs, Yosemite, 1870

We are nine thousand feet above the sea.
Our appetites are ravenous.
We eat up a sheep a day,
roll ourselves in damp blankets
by the fire, go to sleep
while the horses forage

and then we go down into the bubbling pool
of carbonate soda, past limestone
and the bloody aureole of iron,
past the igneous intrusion
of the glacial slide

into the subterranean lake
that lifts now like a mirror

between ourselves and the great plains
of unfossilized crustaceans.

Gila monsters, hairy mammoths,
and crocodiles cool themselves
in these *pleasant, pungent waters,*
in the ice-cold, tonic springs

that rise now with such abundance
through the airy hole of time.

II. *Marianne Moore at Mount Rainier, Washington, 1922*

Warner and I on the ropes like *conspicuously spotted little horses*
tied together above a crevasse. We're brother and sister,
though we might be skiers on a sea of glass
or a pair of spiders spinning across the snow.
He'll marry soon. We pose at the top of the volcano,
at the very lip of the tunnel of ice.
Inside the abyss, I see ammonite buttons and whalebone
corsets and other domestic devices, such as the broom and the
   piano.
I see marriage and I see the mind like *an octopus of ice*
deceptively reserved and flat above the hairline cracks
and tentacles of experience. I take his arm,
as if to say, "Warner, look
down, or for God's sake look up!"
He does nothing of the kind, he looks
straight ahead into an avalanche of falling powder
while down below, a mountain goat scrambles along a moraine,
its eye fixed on a waterfall which never seems to fall.

III. At the Bomb Shelter Expo with My Father, Philadelphia, 1962

The sky is full of objects: satellites, Soviet apparatchiks
in parachutes, their Baltic faces charred as steaks,
their proletarian suits ballooning oddly on the horizon.
We've seen the pictures from the U2s,
missile sites and ammo cases on the beaches
of the Copacabana Hotel, close-ups
of Fidel's caterpillar eyebrows.
Fidel stubs out his cigar
in the eye of Miami's all-night salsa clubs.
Miami, Miami!
City of runaway Cubans
cruising the night away in big American cars.

Real Cubans drive Russian cars, and that's the difference,
you say, far underground in the polyvinyl bunker we can't afford.
It has everything: space blankets, bubble beds,
shelves of canned ravioli and creamed corn.
I take your hand. It wouldn't be so bad
to wait out the war in a nuclear igloo.
I'd read by flashlight, we'd play Monopoly
and listen to the radio, the big bands, Glenn Miller's
"Begin the Beguine," dance cheek to cheek,
my saddle shoes trailing your wingtips across the floor.

Stay. We're deep in the shelter of 1962.
Nothing can happen to me here.
Nothing can happen to you.

III

Songs Against Ending

Monday Music

Nobody, no one, not one, not a single one
hears me at the piano playing the white keys.

I make a truant sound.
I am as eloquent as anything

I heard in the world on Sunday.

Do you remember those conversations?
Accidental, repetitious as language in dreams?

I wonder why it is I know so little
about the black keys,

how they marry and come apart
in the history of a scherzo

or in the history of a scene
in which I play myself

playing only the white keys.

Sometimes I write myself
into a sheet of music

using the usual notations,
my little signs and jokes

of self disappearing.

White, white paperwhites
bloom in winter.

There are birches outside the house.
White crocuses in the snow.

The house is white too.

Above the door, on the lintel,
someone's carved the words

Monday Music Club 1912.

Before the first war happened and the other wars,
the door swings open on its iron hinge

and there's no one at the piano,

nobody I tell you,

as the door swings open.

Eight Pieces for Gertrude Stein

there is no there there
in Oakland California
plums there are plums there

bees's bottoms fruit flies
when Ida comes then she comes
there where the plums lie

to be honey soon
sweetness splits where Ida sits
and where Ida spoons

honey for baby
honey for bees and being
is enough maybe

mere being in time
no there there only this now
this glisten this shine

and listen, Ida,
six, yes there are six senses
in this aria

cuckoo bird sings it
plum tree brings it stumbling down
ripe ripe ripe with it

light-riven girlspun
plum tree summer Ida me
Ida me Ida

Songs Against Ending

I. The Fruit Flies

Spinning lazily in the late sun, they hazard a surmise

The earth's sweet updraft this delicious death ascends

All things fall but some things rise:

                                                           sap, wings, the mote of light
in which the sweet pistil drifts like sugar on a string
also dust, to which sour humanness clings
and resinous musk, rotting tamarind
all that has been peeled back
all that has dissolved
or crystallized

How lovely to sip it

How lovely to sip it first with the prehensile mind

It comes in time
doesn't it

So why not wait and why not spin

Why not wait for it

II. *The Worm*

As she turns, she's pink as any inside girl
and then she's a boy and coiled and phallic

in the soil and she's sex without difference

sex which is moistness
sex which is beauty and fear

She's the perfect female and the perfect male

and as she slips she's sliding
into him and he's eliding into her
sex which is one sex and the same sex
and two sexes at the same time

Then sex lies still for three days in the garden
with another that is like itself but not itself
making a froth there, a bubbling slime
the transference of spermatozoa
each to each into the other

enough, they say, for five sets of hearts
each entranced in its segment

hearts enough to bear the cut
of selves or cells

the accidental wound

the severance

III. The Water Beetle

Old lumberer, father, lonely intruder

helmeted and hermetic
absurd as Agamemnon in your armature

how I fear cracking your skull
one night in the cellar

Why do you favor darkness?
Why are you kin, bachelor?

I know you're there
bearing the weight of your body

the shield and purpose of all your wandering

in this damp traverse
this world we share

IV. The Moths

Late October, they hurry in
just before the rains begin

and they make themselves obscure against a wall

flattening in place like onion skins

or glassy flakes of coal
split off in sheets of fossil darkness

Furred brown or opalescent
seeking heat but not your heat

they pretend to be dead

until one day they are
more dead than pretending

folding in on themselves in a gesture
we recognize as a kind of clinging

to the consolation of form

Interlude with Night Cows, Amherst, Virginia

A soft furred rip, an orison
the earth drives out of herself

as, slowly, the hundred brushes
of their tongues and lips

sweep the gold grasses
into the dark core,

the cave of sentience.

Here, one is merely
animal, beast, hide-bound, nameless

in the calm between hungers
and breeding and deliverance.

The wind shifts its heat,
the breath rises

out of the body
as if body were night

as if body were pasture
and breath were the grammar

of what is.

For Denise Levertov

It is a humming of arrested light

like listening to the listener

then a scattershot, starlings
crowding in the orange tree,

jostling, making much of morning
pouring through the glossy leaves,

the small white blossoms'
essence of sweetness

so concentrated
with love

that all of the pain of your life
breaks apart in that light

as if it were yourself dissolving

White Page of Winter

for Maurine Stuart

I

    Walking home tonight after snow
    nothing but the marks of deer

    crossing one by one
    into a snowy hollow

    The traces of their hooves disappear

    into white sky, white trees
    white slope of ground between the trees

    Never such silence anywhere

II

    When you live with silence
    and the cold white page of winter

    you live awhile with a cold heart

    A cold heart must keep still
    It must learn the content of winter

    It must stand apart
    It must not take shelter

    Can you live awhile with a cold heart?

III

The snowy owl will appear to you
as it lifts out of the topmost branches

and its face in the smoky light
will seem for a moment incandescent

as flame burning a hole through the heart

and for moment it will recognize you
as if you too were light

lifting, lifting out of the dark

Wild Animals I Have Known

for Sue Johnson's Alternate Encyclopedia

I. Frog Prince No. 2

A prince is a man in a frog suit.
A woman is a lure in the shape of a hook.
I favor fringe, the soft effect of fabric over steel.
I like pretty hooks and feathers. I like the feminine deal.

The world is a green pool for fishergirls.
The bed is your mollusk, your thirsty shell.
Drink, little fishergirl, drink.
The pool is your heaven and it is your hell.

He will always leap and you will always lure.
A romance is a story in the shape of a hook.
A fishergirl baits her line with a feathery tip.
A fishergirl drags him up from the green pool

into her mollusk bed, into her thirsty shell,
into her heaven or is it her hell?
Think, little fishergirl, think.
Will you keep him when you catch him?
Will you let him go?

II. The Ugly Duckling

So freakish, the immanent beauty of my inside parts,
my pods and coils, my secret life.

The change, they call it: child into girl,
girl into woman, then woman waking ripe,

waxing cold, bursting hot as a chile in the flame
of what the postmoderns call a situation.

My situation's private, like a goiter no one sees.
There's a seedpod swelling in my throat

and I speak differently than I did before the change.
I speak from here, where pressure blooms

out of me like a baby or like a sac
of meaning and what I want to say

is that I am not what I was. I am
a changeling, half-creaturely,

half other-than-creature,
like a mind inside a body

or like a coil inside a girl,
her sleeping snake, her phallic shape

waking into utterance. Come close. Closer.
I want to tell you everything my body knows.

III. The Clone Lover

It is everything at once, an arrangement
of parts, a sort of mesh

of like into unlike, same into same,
body into nature, nature into

the picture of nature. Your abstract love
fits me, darling, like hand in glove.

Oh, let me imitate your tongue and groove.
I want to leave your imprint everywhere,

you as I imagined you and you as you were
in the real where we subsisted, lover and beloved.

But is it love, this imitation I reproduce as wonder,
my desire to compact and compress

your parts against my parts, my desire
to have you whole or anyway configured

as my other part, my mirror?
If I should move, would you move with me?

Would you dance with me? Would you be my shadow?
Would you be everything at once, an arrangement

of parts into my parts, my lover, my beloved,
my sister, my brother, my other, my one?

IV. The Home of the Hydromedusa

I was in the rapture of the deep with my own kind
and I was floating, floating on a saline tide
inside the lap and flow of pleasure.

I was deep inside the aperture,
an opening of the body and the mind
to the hidden structure. I was in the rapture of the deep.

I was inside the lap and flow of pleasure.
Diatoms sparkled in the nightpools of the sea
and I was a diatom and so was she and we were floating,

floating on a saline tide inside the hidden structure.
I could see the crystalline geometry of the diatom
and of the nightpool and all the stars, the same pattern!

Rock crystal, salt, star, sea, deep in the rapture
of the hidden structure of the body and the mind,
floating, floating inside the lap and flow of pleasure.

V. Paul Bunyan and His Blue Ox, Babe

She's a big girl, Babe, big as a wilderness
or the Great Plains or the tall pines of Coeur d'Alene, Idaho.
She's buff and strong as any woman or any man
and she's my America, made like me out of the same idea.

Babe's pretty horns curl up like the handlebars of my mustache.
She plants her hooves and I plant my boots on a fresh landscape
of smoky stumps, new-cut from the interior forest of a Northern
    plateau.
As I smoke my pipe and regard the effect of a good day's work
    with an ax,
she regards it too out of her sloe eye, the eye she turns toward
    the world.

With an ox like Babe by your side anything's possible and so we
    travel.
We're too big for the bus. We take the shuttle to Cape
    Canaveral
to watch the rockets, then venture north to the heart of Venture
    Capital.
On our way to Europe, we build the Panama Canal.
Babe's got an eye for architecture, likes the sight of skyscrapers,
likes to go first class into the future, into the past.

Together we forge rivers with Pierre the Voyager,
herd buffalo with the Indian Killer, Buffalo Bill.
Many men wanted her but she chose me.
At night, I lie down beside her thick blue fur,
nuzzle her soft snout, and whisper, Babe, Babe,
stay with me. And she stays with me, that's the miracle

of love that we call history. You know the story.
I am a gentle man. She is my wife, my faithful ox.
It is an alternative lifestyle, to be sure.
But who among you dares to judge a love so pure?

Scattered Remnant: The Altamont, California

AFTER STEVE REICH

Push push push the unraveling line. Hasten it, hasten it.

The Altamont's raving with windmills, cows, the semi's grind-
ing climb out of the despised San Joaquin.

Drive out of it.

Drive south to the breach cut like a Y across the impassable
   pass west.
You belong to it. Put it under your tongue. This is speed.

The electric road.

It makes you hum doesn't it, the way you live so fast.

You're connected.

You've got to make it last. You've got to get through.

Otherwise you're just drifting
the way the boy drifts away from his body

under blue tarp, under hawks wheeling
above the car's flipped chassis, the car wheels spinning

and sheared to bits but still moving in place

like us moving   like us moving in place.

The dead boy in the wreck at the side of the road.

Don't you see him drifting?

For fear of losing for fear of being late   for fear of foreclosure
  for fear
of creating the perception of being second rate, of being merely
  present when in fact I am elated   when in fact I am composed
I live for this staggering real   this body blow

The slide home through oleanders dividing east- and westbound
  lanes
the glaze of the windshield dividing me from the scattered
  remnant
the archaeological drift of our last conversation
the letters of our words unraveling

becoming winged and singed as cinders
becoming in time another kind of damage

inscrutable to anyone other than one or two people
though beautiful as a mote of light on a freeway surface

just there, at the center of spun sugar
pulled and pulled and pulled around a stick

There where the shine
sticks to the road you find the line

and you follow it

Hush

The canal murmurs
between inlet and inlet
Fish slip through the nets

irradiated
blue magnetic hybrid fish
swishing through poison-

ous sludge, underground
cables humming metrical
volts, measures, pleasures

like minimalist
compositions scored to re-
peat, repeat, repeat

the pulse of machines
the pulse of our desiring
to live in machines

How can I tell you
You who have made this music
are altered by it

you on the shore, you
who cannot slip through the nets
murmurous, sleepless

you who lie awake
forgetting the names of things
once violently possessed

Night Swimming

Night swimming's mostly a solitary
passage through sidereal time.

Midheaven's above
as the waters lap and close.

Little sac.
I've disappeared without a trace.

What's love if not a waiting to be seen?
What's love if not an opening

of attention, so that it seems sometimes
as if I can see through my skin

how she'll kick out of a lane,
lifting her shoulders into starlight.

Into moonlight? Her dark hair glittering?

I like to look at her
agate-colored eyes, her skin

like olives. Will I ever see her
without needing to be seen?

Will I ever see her whole?

Earth opens into red clay.
Chickweed's sharp and acrid.

In the tall meadow grasses
cicadas rock the night in waves

and I think, *love, love.*

Notes

"Index of Prohibited Images": Much of the background information on Caravaggio and his paintings comes from Peter Robb's *M: The Man Who Became Caravaggio*. The phrases "an obscure, dead wilderness" and "by which we insinuate ourselves/into the contours of the bodies to come" are reworkings of Robb's language. I am indebted, in a number of other poems, such as "Camera Obscura," to Robb's description of Renaissance optics and visual techniques. Robb writes that "in 1597 Cardinal Paleotti urged the compiling of an *Index of prohibited images*, along the lines of the vigorously policed and highly effective *Index of prohibited books*." The Church patronage system, however, was such an excellent censor that the index of prohibited images was never necessary. In "Judith and Holofernes," the phrase from Bob Dylan is from his song "Just Like a Woman," copyright 2000 Sony Music Entertainment Inc. "Medusa" echoes the conclusion of Marguerite Duras's *The Lover* (*L'Amant*), translated from the French by Barbara Bray.

"Corruption": The Robert Lowell line in the epigraph to "The Monsters" is from his poem "Florence." San Marco in "The Saints" refers to the Church of San Marco in Florence.

"Savonarola's Cape": Savonarola's effects are kept in the Cloister of San Marco in Florence, now the Museum of San Marco.

"Three Slaves by Michelangelo Buonarroti": The quotation in "The Awakening Slave" ("But wisdom lies in the awakening of the entire soul/from the slumber of its private wants and opinions") is from Heraclitus.

"Atlas": The poem owes its description of the cervical spine to a conversation with Jane Picard, who always gets the metaphors.

"The Ideal City": The phrase "a systematic display of single point perspective" is quoted from James H. Beck's *Italian Renaissance Painting*. The sentence "When a woman starts up from the sensible world . . . she should not look back/at all she used to love" is an echo of Diotima's dialogue with Socrates in Plato's *Symposium*. The statement "Nobody here, nothing to do" was repeated frequently by Maurine Stuart in her teachings at the Cambridge Zen Buddhist Association, on Sparks Street, in the late 1980s. Maurine Stuart was a Zen Master in the Japanese Rinzai tradition.

"Paradise": The story of Cortés and the Horse of Tayasal appears in Claude Baudez and Sydney Picasso's *Lost Cities of the Maya*.

"Incomprehensible Triangles" was the title of a series of paintings by the South African painter Jo Smail, on view at the Virginia Center for the Creative Arts in the summer of 2003. When I asked her about the title, Smails said that it had been inspired by the writing of Hélène Cixous and Clarice Lispector. She gave me the quotation from Lispector's *The Hour of the Star* (*A hora da estrela*), translated from the Portuguese by Giovanni Pontiero.

"Aperture": The clause "the branching streams flow in the darkness" is from the title of Shunryu Suzuki's *Branching Streams Flow in the Darkness: Zen Talks on the Sandokai,* edited by Mel Weitsman and Michael Wenger.

"Subterranean": The italicized lines in "Joseph Le Conte at Soda Springs, Yosemite, 1870" are from Joseph Le Conte's *Journal of Ramblings Through the High Sierras of California* (High Sierra Classics Series, Yosemite National Park, Calf.: Yosemite Association, 1994).

The italicized phrases in "Marianne Moore at Mount Rainier, Washington, 1922" are from Moore's poem "An Octopus."

"Wild Animals I Have Known" was commissioned by the artist Sue Johnson for her exhibition, the Alternate Encyclopedia, at the Tweed Museum of Art, University of Minnesota, Duluth, in 2004.